A Tale of Three Lions

A Tale of Three Lions

H. Rider Haggard

WAKING LION PRESS

ISBN 978-1-60096-607-1

Published by Waking Lion Press, an imprint of The Editorium

The Editorium, LLC
West Valley City, UT 84128-3917
wakinglionpress.com
wakinglion@editorium.com

Contents

Chapter 1

The Interest on Ten Shillings

Most of you will have heard that Allan Quatermain, who was one of the party that discovered King Solomon's mines some little time ago, and who afterwards came to live in England near his friend Sir Henry Curtis. He went back to the wilderness again, as these old hunters almost invariably do, on one pretext or another.[1] They cannot endure civilization for very long, its noise and racket and the omnipresence of broad-clothed humanity proving more trying to their nerves than the dangers of the desert. I think that they feel lonely here, for it is a fact that is too little understood, though it has often been stated, that there is no loneliness like the loneliness of crowds, especially to those who are unaccustomed to them. "What is there in the world," old Quatermain would say, "so desolate as to stand in the streets of a great city and listen to the footsteps falling, falling, multitudinous as the rain, and watch the white line of faces as they hurry past, you know not whence, you know not whither? They come and go, their eyes meet yours with a cold stare, for a moment their features are written on your mind, and then they are gone for ever. You

---

1. This of course was written before Mr. Quatermain's account of the adventures in the newly-discovered country of Zu-Vendis of himself, Sir Henry Curtis, and Capt. John Good had been received in England.—Editor.

will never see them again; they will never see you again; they come up out of the unknown, and presently they once more vanish into the unknown, taking their secrets with them. Yes, that is loneliness pure and undefiled; but to one who knows and loves it, the wilderness is not lonely, because the spirit of nature is ever there to keep the wanderer company. He finds companions in the winds—the sunny streams babble like Nature's children at his feet; high above them, in the purple sunset, are domes and minarets and palaces, such as no mortal man has built, in and out of whose flaming doors the angels of the sun seem to move continually. And there, too, is the wild game, following its feeding-grounds in great armies, with the springbuck thrown out before for skirmishers; then rank upon rank of long-faced blesbuck, marching and wheeling like infantry; and last the shining troops of quagga, and the fierce-eyed shaggy vilderbeeste to take, as it were, the place of the cossack host that hangs upon an army's flanks.

"Oh, no," he would say, "the wilderness is not lonely, for, my boy, remember that the further you get from man, the nearer you grow to God," and though this is a saying that might well be disputed, it is one I am sure that anybody will easily understand who has watched the sun rise and set on the limitless deserted plains, and seen the thunder chariots of the clouds roll in majesty across the depths of unfathomable sky.

Well, at any rate we went back again, and now for many months I have heard nothing at all of him, and to be frank, I greatly doubt if anybody will ever hear of him again. I fear that the wilderness, that has for so many years been a mother to him, will now also prove his grave and the grave of those who accompanied him, for the quest upon which he and they have started is a wild one indeed.

But while he was in England for those three years or so between his return from the successful discovery of the wise king's buried treasures, and the death of his only son, I saw a great deal of old Allan Quatermain. I had known him years before in Africa, and after he came home, whenever I had nothing better to do, I used to run up to Yorkshire and stay with him, and in this way I at one time and another heard many of the incidents of his past life, and most curious some of them were. No man can pass all those years following the rough existence of an elephant-hunter without meeting with many strange adventures, and in one way and another old Quatermain has certainly seen his share. Well, the story that I am going to tell you in the following pages is one of the later of these adventures, though I forget the exact year in which it happened. at any rate I know that it was the only trip upon which he took his son Harry (who is since dead) with him, and that Harry was then about fourteen. And now for the story, which I will repeat, as nearly as I can, in the words in which Hunter Quatermain told it to me one night in the old oak-panelled vestibule of his house in Yorkshire. We were talking about gold- mining—

"Gold-mining!" he broke in; "ah! yes, I once went gold-mining at Pilgrims' Rest in the Transvaal, and it was after that that we had the business about Jim-Jim and the lions. Do you know Pilgrim's Rest? Well, it is, or was, one of the queerest little places you ever saw. The town itself was pitched in a stony valley, with mountains all about it, and in the middle of such scenery as one does not often get the chance of seeing. Many and many is the time that I have thrown down my pick and shovel in disgust, clambered out of my claim, and walked a couple of miles or so to the top of some hill. Then I would lie down in the grass and look out over the glorious stretch of country—the smiling valleys, the great mountains touched with gold—real gold of the sunset, and clothed in sweeping robes of bush, and stare into the depths of the perfect sky above; yes, and thank Heaven I had got away from the cursing and the coarse jokes of the miners, and the voices of those

3

Basutu Kaffirs as they toiled in the sun, the memory of which is with me yet.

"Well, for some months I dug away patiently at my claim, till the very sight of a pick or of a washing-trough became hateful to me. A hundred times a day I lamented my own folly in having invested eight hundred pounds, which was about all that I was worth at the time, in this gold-mining. But like other better people before me, I had been bitten by the gold bug, and now was forced to take the consequences. I bought a claim out of which a man had made a fortune—five or six thousand pounds at least—as I thought, very cheap; that is, I gave him five hundred pounds down for it. It was all that I had made by a very rough year's elephant-hunting beyond the Zambesi, and I sighed deeply and prophetically when I saw my successful friend, who was a Yankee, sweep up the roll of Standard Bank notes with the lordly air of the man who has made his fortune, and cram them into his breeches pockets. 'Well,' I said to him—the happy vendor—'it is a magnificent property, and I only hope that my luck will be as good as yours has been.'

"He smiled; to my excited nerves it seemed that he smiled ominously, as he answered me in a peculiar Yankee drawl: 'I guess, stranger, as I ain't the one to make a man quarrel with his food, more especial when there ain't no more going of the rounds; and as for that there claim, well, she's been a good nigger to me; but between you and me, stranger, speaking man to man, now that there ain't any filthy lucre between us to obscure the features of the truth, I guess she's about worked out!'

"I gasped; the fellow's effrontery took the breath out of me. Only five minutes before he had been swearing by all his gods—and they appeared to be numerous and mixed—that there were half a dozen fortunes left in the claim, and that he was only giving it up because he was downright weary of shovelling the gold out.

"'Don't look so vexed, stranger,' went on my tormentor, 'perhaps there is some shine in the old girl yet; anyway you are a downright good fellow, you are, therefore you will, I guess, have a real A1 opportunity of working on the feelings of Fortune. Anyway it will bring the muscle up upon your arm, for the stuff is uncommon stiff, and, what is more, you will in the course of a year earn a sight more than two thousand dollars in value of experience.'

"Then he went just in time, for in another moment I should have gone for him, and I saw his face no more.

"Well, I set to work on the old claim with my boy Harry and half a dozen Kaffirs to help me, which, seeing that I had put nearly all my worldly wealth into it, was the least that I could do. And we worked, my word, we did work—early and late we went at it—but never a bit of gold did we see; no, not even a nugget large enough to make a scarf- pin out of. The American gentleman had secured it all and left us the sweepings.

"For three months this went on, till at last I had paid away all, or very near all, that was left of her little capital in wages and food for the Kaffirs and ourselves. When I tell you that Boer meal was sometimes as high as four pounds a bag, you will understand that it did not take long to run through our banking account.

"At last the crisis came. One Saturday night I had paid the men as usual, and bought a muid of mealie meal at sixty shillings for them to fill themselves with, and then I went with my boy Harry and sat on the edge of the great hole that we had dug in the hill-side, and which we had in bitter mockery named Eldorado. There we sat in the moonlight with our feet over the edge of the claim, and were melancholy enough for anything. Presently I pulled out my purse and emptied its contents into my hand. There was a half-sovereign, two florins, ninepence in silver, no coppers—for copper practically does not circulate in South Africa, which is one of the things that make living so dear there—in all exactly fourteen and ninepence.

"'There, Harry, my boy!' I said, 'that is the sum total of our worldly wealth; that hole has swallowed all the rest.'

"'By George!' said Master Harry; 'I say, father, you and I shall have to let ourselves out to work with the Kaffirs and live on mealie pap,' and he sniggered at his unpleasant little joke.

"But I was in no mood for joking, for it is not a merry thing to dig like anything for months and be completely ruined in the process, especially if you happen to dislike digging, and consequently I resented Harry's light-heartedness.

"'Be quiet, boy!' I said, raising my hand as though to give him a cuff, with the result that the half-sovereign slipped out of it and fell into the gulf below.

"'Oh, bother,' said I, 'it's gone.'

"'There, Dad,' said Harry, 'that's what comes of letting your angry passions rise; now we are down to four and nine.'

"I made no answer to these words of wisdom, but scrambled down the steep sides of the claim, followed by Harry, to hunt for my little all. Well, we hunted and we hunted, but the moonlight is an uncertain thing to look for half-sovereigns by, and there was some loose soil about, for the Kaffirs had knocked off working at this very spot a couple of hours before. I took a pick and raked away the clods of earth with it, in the hope of finding the coin; but all in vain. At last in sheer annoyance I struck the sharp end of the pickaxe down into the soil, which was of a very hard nature. To my astonishment it sunk in right up to the haft.

"'Why, Harry,' I said, 'this ground must have been disturbed!'

"'I don't think so, father,' he answered; 'but we will soon see,' and he began to shovel out the soil with his hands. 'Oh,' he said presently, 'it's only some old stones; the pick has gone down between them, look!' and he began to pull at one of the stones.

"'I say, Dad,' he said presently, almost in a whisper, 'it's precious heavy, feel it;' and he rose and gave me a round, brownish lump about the size of a very large apple, which he was holding in both his hands. I took it curiously and held it up to the light. It /was/ very heavy. The moonlight fell upon its rough and filth-encrusted surface, and as I looked, curious little thrills of excitement began to pass through me. But I could not be sure.

"'Give me your knife, Harry,' I said.

"He did so, and resting the brown stone on my knee I scratched at its surface. Great heavens, it was soft!

"Another second and the secret was out, we had found a great nugget of pure gold, four pounds of it or more. 'It's gold, lad,' I said, 'it's gold, or I'm a Dutchman!'

"Harry, with his eyes starting out of his head, glared down at the gleaming yellow scratch that I had made upon the virgin metal, and then burst out into yell upon yell of exultation, which went ringing away across the silent claims like shrieks of somebody being murdered.

"'Be quiet!' I said; 'do you want every thief on the fields after you?'

"Scarcely were the words out of my mouth when I heard a stealthy footstep approaching. I promptly put the big nugget down and sat on it, and uncommonly hard it was. As I did so I saw a lean dark face poked over the edge of the claim and a pair of beady eyes searching us out. I knew the face, it belonged to a man of very bad character known as Handspike Tom, who had, I understood, been so named at the Diamond Fields because he had murdered his mate with a handspike. He was now no doubt prowling about like a human hyæna to see what he could steal.

"'Is that you, 'unter Quatermain?' he said.

"'Yes, it's I, Mr. Tom,' I answered, politely.

"'And what might all that there yelling be?' he asked. 'I was walking along, a-taking of the evening air and a-thinking on the stars, when I 'ears 'owl after 'owl.'

"'Well, Mr. Tom,' I answered, 'that is not to be wondered at, seeing that like yourself they are nocturnal birds.'

"'"Owl after 'owl!' he repeated sternly, taking no notice of my interpretation, 'and I stops and says, "That's murder," and I listens again and thinks, "No, it ain't; that 'owl is the 'owl of hexultation; some one's been and got his fingers into a gummy yeller pot, I'll swear, and gone off 'is 'ead in the sucking of them." Now, 'unter Quatermain, is I right? is it nuggets? Oh, lor!' and he smacked his lips audibly—'great big yellow boys— is it them that you have just been and tumbled across?'

"'No,' I said boldly, 'it isn't'—the cruel gleam in his black eyes altogether overcoming my aversion to untruth, for I knew that if once he found out what it was that I was sitting on—and by the way I have heard of rolling in gold being spoken of as a pleasant process, but I certainly do not recommend anybody who values comfort to try sitting on it—I should run a very good chance of being 'handspiked' before the night was over.

"'If you want to know what it was, Mr. Tom,' I went on, with my politest air, although in agony from the nugget underneath—for I hold it is always best to be polite to a man who is so ready with a handspike—'my boy and I have had a slight difference of opinion, and I was enforcing my view of the matter upon him; that's all.'

"'Yes, Mr. Tom,' put in Harry, beginning to weep, for Harry was a smart boy, and saw the difficulty we were in, 'that was it—I halloed because father beat me.'

"'Well, now, did yer, my dear boy—did yer? Well, all I can say is that a played-out old claim is a wonderful queer sort of place to come to for to argify at ten o'clock of night, and what's more, my sweet youth, if ever I should 'ave the argifying of yer'—and he leered unpleasantly at Harry—'yer won't 'oller in quite such a jolly sort 'o way. And now I'll be saying good-night, for I don't like disturbing of a family party. No, I ain't that sort of man, I ain't. Good-night to yer, 'unter Quatermain—good-night to yer, my argified young one;' and Mr. Tom turned away disappointed, and prowled off elsewhere, like a human jackal, to see what he could thieve or kill.

"'Thank goodness!' I said, as I slipped off the lump of gold. 'Now, then, do you get up, Harry, and see if that consummate villain has gone.' Harry did so, and reported that he had vanished towards Pilgrim's Rest, and then we set to work, and very carefully, but trembling with excitement, with our hands hollowed out all the space of ground into which I had struck the pick. Yes, as I hoped, there was a regular nest of nuggets, twelve in all, running from the size of a hazel-nut to that of a hen's egg, though of course the first one was much larger than that. How they all came there nobody can say; it was one of those extraordinary freaks, with stories of which, at any rate, all people acquainted with alluvial gold-mining will be familiar. It turned out afterwards that the American who sold me the claim had in the same way made his pile—a much larger one than ours, by the way—out of a single pocket, and then worked for six months without seeing colour, after which he gave it up.

"At any rate, there the nuggets were, to the value, as it turned out afterwards, of about twelve hundred and fifty pounds, so that after all I took out of that hole four hundred and fifty pounds more than I put into it. We got them all out and wrapped them up in a handkerchief, and then, fearing to carry home so much treasure, especially as we knew that Mr. Handspike Tom was on the prowl, made up our minds to pass the night where we were—a necessity which, disagreeable as it was, was wonderfully sweetened by the presence of that handkerchief full of virgin gold—the interest of my lost half-sovereign.

"Slowly the night wore away, for with the fear of Handspike Tom before my eyes I did not dare to go to sleep, and at last the dawn came. I got up and watched its growth, till it opened like a flower upon the eastern sky, and the sunbeams began to spring up in splendour from mountain-top to mountain-top. I watched it, and as I did so it flashed upon me, with a complete conviction which I had not felt before, that I had had enough of gold-mining to last me the rest of my natural life, and I then and there made up my mind to clear out of Pilgrims' Rest and go and shoot buffalo towards Delagoa Bay. Then I turned, took the pick and shovel, and although it was a Sunday morning, woke up Harry and set to work to see if there were any more nuggets about. As I expected, there were none. What we had got had lain together in a little pocket filled with soil that felt quite different from the stiff stuff round and outside the pocket. There was not another trace of gold. Of course it is possible that there were more pocketfuls somewhere about, but all I have to say is I made up my mind that, whoever found them, I should not; and, as a matter of fact, I have since heard that this claim has been the ruin of two or three people, as it very nearly was the ruin of me.

"'Harry,' I said presently, 'I am going away this week towards Delagoa to shoot buffalo. Shall I take you with me, or send you down to Durban?'

"'Oh, take me with you, father!' begged Harry, 'I want to kill a buffalo!'

"'And supposing that the buffalo kills you instead?' I asked.

"'Oh, never mind,' he said, gaily, 'there are lots more where I came from.'

"I rebuked him for his flippancy, but in the end I consented to take him.

Chapter 2

What Was Found in the Pool

"Something over a fortnight had passed since the night when I lost half-a-sovereign and found twelve hundred and fifty pounds in looking for it, and instead of that horrid hole, for which, after all, Eldorado was hardly a misnomer, a very different scene stretched away before us clad in the silver robe of the moonlight. We were camped—Harry and I, two Kaffirs, a Scotch cart, and six oxen—on the swelling side of a great wave of bushclad land. Just where we had made our camp, however, the bush was very sparse, and only grew about in clumps, while here and there were single flat-topped mimosa-trees. To our right a little stream, which had cut a deep channel for itself in the bosom of the slope, flowed musically on between banks green with maidenhair, wild asparagus, and many beautiful grasses. The bed-rock here was red granite, and in the course of centuries of patient washing the water had hollowed out some of the huge slabs in its path into great troughs and cups, and these we used for bathing-places. No Roman lady, with her baths of porphyry or alabaster, could have had a more delicious spot to bathe herself than we found within fifty yards of our skerm, or rough inclosure of mimosa thorn, that we had dragged together round the cart to protect us from the attacks of lions. That there were several of these brutes about, I knew from their spoor, though we had neither heard nor seen them.

"Our bath was a little nook where the eddy of the stream had washed away a mass of soil, and on the edge of it there grew a most beautiful old mimosa thorn. Beneath the thorn was a large smooth slab of granite fringed all round with maidenhair and other ferns, that sloped gently down to a pool of the clearest sparkling water, which lay in a bowl of granite about ten feet wide by five feet deep in the centre. Here to this slab we went every morning to bathe, and that delightful bath is among the most pleasant of my hunting reminiscences, as it is also, for reasons which will presently appear, among the most painful.

"It was a lovely night. Harry and I sat to the windward of the fire, where the two Kaffirs were busily employed in cooking some impala steaks off a buck which Harry, to his great joy, had shot that morning, and were as perfectly contented with ourselves and the world at large as two people could possibly be. The night was beautiful, and it would require somebody with more words on the tip of his tongue than I have to describe properly the chastened majesty of those moonlit wilds. Away for ever and for ever, away to the mysterious north, rolled the great bush ocean over which the silence brooded. There beneath us a mile or more to the right ran the wide Oliphant, and mirror-like flashed back the moon, whose silver spears were shivered on its breast, and then tossed in twisted lines of light far and wide about the mountains and the plain. Down upon the river-banks grew great timber-trees that through the stillness pointed solemnly to Heaven, and the beauty of the night lay upon them like a cloud. Everywhere was silence—silence in the starred depths, silence on the bosom of the sleeping earth. Now, if ever, great thoughts might rise in a man's mind, and for a space he might forget his littleness in the sense that he partook of the pure immensity about him.

"'Hark! what was that?'

"From far away down by the river there comes a mighty rolling sound, then another, and another. It is the lion seeking his meat.

"I saw Harry shiver and turn a little pale. He was a plucky boy enough, but the roar of a lion heard for the first time in the solemn bush veldt at night is apt to shake the nerves of any lad.

"'Lions, my boy,' I said; 'they are hunting down by the river there; but I don't think that you need make yourself uneasy. We have been here three nights now, and if they were going to pay us a visit I think that they would have done so before this. However, we will make up the fire.'

"'Here, Pharaoh, do you and Jim-Jim get some more wood before we go to sleep, else the cats will be purring round you before morning.'

"Pharaoh, a great brawny Swazi, who had been working for me at Pilgrims' Rest, laughed, rose, and stretched himself, then calling to Jim-Jim to bring the axe and a reim, started off in the moonlight towards a clump of sugar-bush where we cut our fuel from some dead trees. He was a fine fellow in his way, was Pharaoh, and I think that he had been named Pharaoh because he had an Egyptian cast of countenance and a royal sort of swagger about him. But his way was a somewhat peculiar way, on account of the uncertainty of his temper, and very few people could get on with him; also if he could find liquor he would drink like a fish, and when he drank he became shockingly bloodthirsty. These were his bad points; his good ones were that, like most people of the Zulu blood, he became exceedingly attached if he took to you at all; he was a hard-working and intelligent man, and about as dare-devil and plucky a fellow at a pinch as I have ever had to do with. He was about five-and-thirty years of age or so, but not a 'keshla' or ringed man. I believe that he had got into trouble in some way in Swaziland, and the authorities of his

13

tribe would not allow him to assume the ring, and that is why he came to work at the gold-fields. The other man, or rather lad, Jim- Jim, was a Mapoch Kaffir, or Knobnose, and even in the light of subsequent events I fear I cannot speak very well of him. He was an idle and careless young rascal, and only that very morning I had to tell Pharaoh to give him a beating for letting the oxen stray, which Pharaoh did with the greatest gusto, although he was by way of being very fond of Jim-Jim. Indeed, I saw him consoling Jim-Jim afterwards with a pinch of snuff from his own ear-box, whilst he explained to him that the next time it came in the way of duty to flog him, he meant to thrash him with the other hand, so as to cross the old cuts and make a "pretty pattern" on his back.

"Well, off they went, though Jim-Jim did not at all like leaving the camp at that hour, even when the moonlight was so bright, and in due course returned safely enough with a great bundle of wood. I laughed at Jim-Jim, and asked him if he had seen anything, and he said yes, he had; he had seen two large yellow eyes staring at him from behind a bush, and heard something snore.

"As, however, on further investigation the yellow eyes and the snore appeared to have existed only in Jim-Jim's lively imagination, I was not greatly disturbed by this alarming report; but having seen to the making-up of the fire, got into the skerm and went quietly to sleep with Harry by my side.

"Some hours afterwards I woke up with a start. I don't know what woke me. The moon had gone down, or at least was almost hidden behind the soft horizon of bush, only her red rim being visible. Also a wind had sprung up and was driving long hurrying lines of cloud across the starry sky, and altogether a great change had come over the mood of the night. By the look of the sky I judged that we must be about two hours from day-break.

"The oxen, which were as usual tied to the disselboom of the Scotch cart, were very restless—they kept snuffling and blowing, and rising up and lying down again, so I at once suspected that they must wind something. Presently I knew what it was that they winded, for within fifty yards of us a lion roared, not very loud, but quite loud enough to make my heart come into my mouth.

"Pharaoh was sleeping on the other side of the cart, and, looking beneath it, I saw him raise his head and listen.

"'Lion, Inkoos,' he whispered, 'lion!'

"Jim-Jim also jumped up, and by the faint light I could see that he was in a very great fright indeed.

"Thinking that it was as well to be prepared for emergencies, I told Pharaoh to throw wood upon the fire, and woke up Harry, who I verily believe was capable of sleeping happily through the crack of doom. He was a little scared at first, but presently the excitement of the position came home to him, and he grew quite anxious to see his majesty face to face. I got my rifle handy and gave Harry his—a Westley Richards falling block, which is a very useful gun for a youth, being light and yet a good killing rifle, and then we waited.

"For a long time nothing happened, and I began to think that the best thing we could do would be to go to sleep again, when suddenly I heard a sound more like a cough than a roar within about twenty yards of the skerm. We all looked out, but could see nothing; and then followed another period of suspense. It was very trying to the nerves, this waiting for an attack that might be developed from any quarter or might not be developed at all; and though I was an old hand at this sort of business I was anxious about Harry, for it is wonderful how the presence of anybody to whom one is attached unnerves a man in moments of danger. I know, although it was now chilly enough, I could feel the perspiration running down my nose, and in order to relieve the strain on my attention employed myself in watching a beetle which appeared to be attracted by the firelight, and was sitting before it thoughtfully rubbing his antennæ against each other.

"Suddenly, the beetle gave such a jump that he nearly pitched headlong into the fire, and so did we all—gave jumps, I mean, and no wonder, for from right under the skerm fence there came a most frightful roar—a roar that literally made the Scotch cart shake and took the breath out of me.

"Harry made an exclamation, Jim-Jim howled outright, while the poor oxen, who were terrified almost out of their hides, shivered and lowed piteously.

"The night was almost entirely dark now, for the moon had quite set, and the clouds had covered up the stars, so that the only light we had came from the fire, which by this time was burning up brightly again. But, as you know, firelight is absolutely useless to shoot by, it is so uncertain, and besides, it penetrates but a very little way into the darkness, although if one is in the dark outside, one can see it from far away.

"Presently the oxen, after standing still for a moment, suddenly winded the lion and did what I feared they would do—began to 'skrek,' that is, to try and break loose from the trektow to which they were tied, to rush off madly into the wilderness. Lions know of this habit on the part of oxen, which are, I do believe, the most foolish animals under the sun, a sheep being a very Solomon compared to them; and it is by no means uncommon for a lion to get in such a position that a herd or span of oxen may wind him, skrek, break their reims, and rush off into the bush. Of course, once there, they are helpless in the dark; and then the lion chooses the one that he loves best and eats him at his leisure.

"Well, round and round went our six poor oxen, nearly trampling us to death in their mad rush; indeed, had we not hastily tumbled out of the way, we should have been trodden to death, or at the least seriously injured. As it was,

Harry was run over, and poor Jim-Jim being caught by the trektow somewhere beneath the arm, was hurled right across the skerm, landing by my side only some paces off.

"Snap went the disselboom of the cart beneath the transverse strain put upon it. Had it not broken the cart would have overset; as it was, in another minute, oxen, cart, trektow, reims, broken disselboom, and everything were soon tied in one vast heaving, plunging, bellowing, and seemingly inextricable knot.

"For a moment or two this state of affairs took my attention off from the lion that had caused it, but whilst I was wondering what on earth was to be done next, and how we should manage if the cattle broke loose into the bush and were lost— for cattle frightened in this manner will so straight away like mad things—my thoughts were suddenly recalled to the lion in a very painful fashion.

"For at that moment I perceived by the light of the fire a kind of gleam of yellow travelling through the air towards us.

"'The lion! the lion!' holloaed Pharaoh, and as he did so, he, or rather she, for it was a great gaunt lioness, half wild no doubt with hunger, lit right in the middle of the skerm, and stood there in the smoky gloom lashing her tail and roaring. I seized my rifle and fired it at her, but what between the confusion, my agitation, and the uncertain light, I missed her, and nearly shot Pharaoh. The flash of the rifle, however, threw the whole scene into strong relief, and a wild sight it was I can tell you—with the seething mass of oxen twisted all round the cart, in such a fashion that their heads looked as though they were growing out of their rumps; and their horns seemed to protrude from their backs; the smoking fire with just a blaze in the heart of the smoke; Jim-Jim in the foreground, where the oxen had thrown him in their wild rush, stretched out there in terror, and then as a centre to the picture the great gaunt lioness glaring round with hungry yellow eyes, roaring and whining as she made up her mind what to do.

17

"It did not take her long, however, just the time that it takes a flash to die into darkness, for, before I could fire again or do anything, with a most fiendish snort she sprang upon poor Jim-Jim.

"I heard the unfortunate lad shriek, and then almost instantly I saw his legs thrown into the air. The lioness had seized him by the neck, and with a sudden jerk thrown his body over her back so that his legs hung down upon the further side.[1] Then, without the slightest hesitation, and apparently without any difficulty, she cleared the skerm face at a single bound, and bearing poor Jim-Jim with her vanished into the darkness beyond, in the direction of the bathing- place that I have already described. We jumped up perfectly mad with horror and fear, and rushed wildly after her, firing shots at haphazard on the chance that she would be frightened by them into dropping her prey, but nothing could we see, and nothing could we hear. The lioness had vanished into the darkness, taking Jim-Jim with her, and to attempt to follow her till daylight was madness. We should only expose ourselves to the risk of a like fate.

"So with scared and heavy hearts we crept back to the skerm, and sat down to wait for the dawn, which now could not be much more than an hour off. It was absolutely useless to try even to disentangle the oxen till then, so all that was left for us to do was to sit and wonder how it came to pass that the one should be taken and the other left, and to hope against hope that our poor servant might have been mercifully delivered from the lion's jaws.

"At length the faint dawn came stealing like a ghost up the long slope of bush, and glinted on the tangled oxen's horns,

---

1. I have known a lion carry a two-year-old ox over a stone wall four feet high in this fashion, and a mile away into the bush beyond. He was subsequently poisoned by strychnine put into the carcass of the ox, and I still have his claws.— Editor.

and with white and frightened faces we got up and set to the task of disentangling the oxen, till such time as there should be light enough to enable us to follow the trail of the lioness which had gone off with Jim-Jim. And here a fresh trouble awaited us, for when at last with infinite difficulty we had disentangled the great helpless brutes, it was only to find that one of the best of them was very sick. There was no mistake about the way he stood with his legs slightly apart and his head hanging down. He had got the redwater, I was sure of it. Of all the difficulties connected with life and travelling in South Africa those connected with oxen are perhaps the worst. The ox is the most exasperating animal in the world, a negro excepted. He has absolutely no constitution, and never neglects an opportunity of falling sick of some mysterious disease. He will get thin upon the slightest provocation, and from mere maliciousness die of 'poverty'; whereas it is his chief delight to turn round and refuse to pull whenever he finds himself well in the centre of a river, or the waggon-wheel nicely fast in a mud hole. Drive him a few miles over rough roads and you will find that he is footsore; turn him loose to feed and you will discover that he has run away, or if he has not run away he has of malice aforethought eaten 'tulip' and poisoned himself. There is always something with him. The ox is a brute. It was of a piece with his accustomed behaviour for the one in question to break out—on purpose probably— with redwater just when a lion had walked off with his herd. It was exactly what I should have expected, and I was therefore neither disappointed nor surprised.

"Well, it was no use crying as I should almost have liked to do, because if this ox had redwater it was probable that the rest of them had it too, although they had been sold to me as 'salted,' that is, proof against such diseases as redwater and lungsick. One gets hardened to this sort of thing in South

Africa in course of time, for I suppose in no other country in the world is the waste of animal life so great.

"So taking my rifle and telling Harry to follow me (for we had to leave Pharaoh to look after the oxen—Pharaoh's lean kine, I called them), I started to see if anything could be found of or appertaining to the unfortunate Jim-Jim. The ground round our little camp was hard and rocky, and we could not hit off any spoor of the lioness, though just outside the skerm was a drop or two of blood. About three hundred yards from the camp, and a little to the right, was a patch of sugar bush mixed up with the usual mimosa, and for this I made, thinking that the lioness would have been sure to take her prey there to devour it. On we pushed through the long grass that was bent down beneath the weight of the soaking dew. In two minutes we were wet through up to the thighs, as wet as though we had waded through water. In due course, however, we reached the patch of bush, and by the grey light of the morning cautiously and slowly pushed our way into it. It was very dark under the trees, for the sun was not yet up, so we walked with the most extreme care, half expecting every minute to come across the lioness licking the bones of poor Jim-Jim. But no lioness could we see, and as for Jim-Jim there was not even a finger-joint of him to be found. Evidently they had not come here.

"So pushing through the bush we proceeded to hunt every other likely spot, but with the same result.

"'I suppose she must have taken him right away,' I said at last, sadly enough. 'At any rate he will be dead by now, so God have mercy on him, we can't help him. What's to be done now?'

"'I suppose that we had better wash ourselves in the pool, and then go back and get something to eat. I am filthy,' said Harry.

"This was a practical if a somewhat unfeeling suggestion. At least it struck me as unfeeling to talk of washing when poor Jim-Jim had been so recently eaten. However, I did not let my sentiment carry me away, so we went down to the beautiful spot that I have described, to wash. I was the first to reach it, which I did by scrambling down the ferny bank. Then I turned round, and started back with a yell—as well I might, for almost from beneath my feet there came a most awful snarl.

"I had lit nearly upon the back of the lioness, that had been sleeping on the slab where we always stood to dry ourselves after bathing. With a snarl and a growl, before I could do anything, before I could even cock my rifle, she had bounded right across the crystal pool, and vanished over the opposite bank. It was all done in an instant, as quick as thought.

"She had been sleeping on the slab, and oh, horror! what was that sleeping beside her? It was the red remains of poor Jim-Jim, lying on a patch of blood-stained rock.

"'Oh! father, father!' shrieked Harry, 'look in the water!'

"I looked. There, floating in the centre of the lovely tranquil pool, was Jim-Jim's head. The lioness had bitten it right off, and it had rolled down the sloping rock into the water.

Chapter 3

Jim-Jim Is Avenged

"We never bathed in that pool again; indeed for my part I could never look at its peaceful purity fringed round with waving ferns without thinking of that ghastly head which rolled itself off through the water when we tried to catch it.

"Poor Jim-Jim! We buried what was left of him, which was not very much, in an old bread-bag, and though whilst he lived his virtues were not great, now that he was gone we could have wept over him. Indeed, Harry did weep outright; while Pharaoh used very bad language in Zulu, and I registered a quiet little vow on my account that I would let daylight into that lioness before I was forty-eight hours older, if by any means it could be done.

"Well, we buried him, and there he lies in the bread-bag (which I rather grudged him, as it was the only one we had), where lions will not trouble him any more—though perhaps the hyænas will, if they consider that there is enough on him left to make it worth their while to dig him up. However, he won't mind that; so there is an end of the book of Jim-Jim.

"The question that now remained was, how to circumvent his murderess. I knew that she would be sure to return as soon as she was hungry again, but I did not know when she would be hungry. She had left so little of Jim-Jim behind her that I should scarcely expect to see her the next night, unless indeed she had cubs. Still, I felt that it would not be wise to miss the chance of her coming, so we set about making preparations for her reception. The first thing that we did was to strengthen the bush wall of the skerm by dragging a large quantity of the tops of thorn-trees together, and laying them one on the other in such a fashion that the thorns pointed outwards. This, after our experience of the fate of Jim-Jim, seemed a very necessary precaution, since if where one goat can jump another can follow, as the Kaffirs say, how much more is this the case when an animal so active and so vigorous as the lion is concerned! And now came the further question, how were we to beguile the lioness to return? Lions are animals that have a strange knack of appearing when they are not wanted, and keeping studiously out of the way when their presence is required. Of course it was possible that if she had found Jim-Jim to her liking she would come back to see if there were any more of his kind about, but still it was not to be relied on.

"Harry, who as I have said was an eminently practical boy, suggested to Pharaoh that he should go and sit outside the skerm in the moonlight as a sort of bait, assuring him that he would have nothing to fear, as we should certainly kill the lioness before she killed him. Pharaoh however, strangely enough, did not seem to take to this suggestion. Indeed, he walked away, much put out with Harry for having made it.

"It gave me an idea, however.

"'By Jove!' I said, 'there is the sick ox. He must die sooner or later, so we may as well utilize him.'

"Now, about thirty yards to the left of our skerm, as one stood facing down the hill towards the river, was the stump of a tree that had been destroyed by lightning many years before, standing equidistant between, but a little in front of, two clumps of bush, which were severally some fifteen paces from it.

24

"Here was the very place to tie the ox; and accordingly a little before sunset the sick animal was led forth by Pharaoh and made fast there, little knowing, poor brute, for what purpose; and we began our long vigil, this time without a fire, for our object was to attract the lioness and not to scare her.

"For hour after hour we waited, keeping ourselves awake by pinching each other—it is, by the way, remarkable what a difference of opinion as to the force of pinches requisite to the occasion exists in the mind of pincher and pinched—but no lioness came. At last the moon went down, and darkness swallowed up the world, as the Kaffirs say, but no lions came to swallow us up. We waited till dawn, because we did not dare to go to sleep, and then at last with many bad thoughts in our hearts we took such rest as we could get, and that was not much.

"That morning we went out shooting, not because we wanted to, for we were too depressed and tired, but because we had no more meat. For three hours or more we wandered about in a broiling sun looking for something to kill, but with absolutely no results. For some unknown reason the game had grown very scarce about the spot, though when I was there two years before every sort of large game except rhinoceros and elephant was particularly abundant. The lions, of whom there were many, alone remained, and I fancy that it was the fact of the game they live on having temporarily migrated which made them so daring and ferocious. As a general rule a lion is an amiable animal enough if he is left alone, but a hungry lion is almost as dangerous as a hungry man. One hears a great many different opinions expressed as to whether or no the lion is remarkable for his courage, but the result of my experience is that very much depends upon the state of his stomach. A hungry lion will not stick at a trifle, whereas a full one will flee at a very small rebuke.

25

"Well, we hunted all about, and nothing could we see, not even a duiker or a bush buck; and at last, thoroughly tired and out of temper, we started on our way back to camp, passing over the brow of a steepish hill to do so. Just as we climbed the crest of the ridge I came to a stand, for there, about six hundred yards to my left, his beautiful curved horns outlined against the soft blue of the sky, I saw a noble koodoo bull (/Strepsiceros kudu/). Even at that distance, for as you know my eyes are very keen, I could distinctly see the white stripes on its side when the light fell upon it, and its large and pointed ears twitch as the flies worried it.

"So far so good; but how were we to get at it? It was ridiculous to risk a shot at that great distance, and yet both the ground and the wind lay very ill for stalking. It seemed to me that the only chance would be to make a detour of at least a mile or more, and come up on the other side of the koodoo. I called Harry to my side, and explained to him what I thought would be our best course, when suddenly, without any delay, the koodoo saved us further trouble by suddenly starting off down the hill like a leaping rocket. I do not know what had frightened it, certainly we had not. Perhaps a hyæna or a leopard—a tiger as we call it there—had suddenly appeared; at any rate, off it went, running slightly towards us, and I never saw a buck go faster. I am afraid that forgetting Harry's presence I used strong language, and really there was some excuse. As for Harry, he stood watching the beautiful animal's course. Presently it vanished behind a patch of bush, to emerge a few seconds later about five hundred paces from us, on a stretch of comparatively level ground that was strewn with boulders. On it went, clearing the boulders in its path with a succession of great bounds that were beautiful to behold. As it did so, I happened to look round at Harry, and perceived to my astonishment that he had got his rifle to his shoulder.

"'You young donkey!' I exclaimed, 'surely you are not going to'—and just at that moment the rifle went off.

"And then I think I saw what was in its way one of the most wonderful things I ever remember in my hunting experience. The koodoo was at the moment in the air, clearing a pile of stones with its fore-legs tucked up underneath it. All of an instant the legs stretched themselves out in a spasmodic fashion, it lit on them, and they doubled up beneath it. Down went the noble buck, down upon his head. For a moment he seemed to be standing on his horns, his hind-legs high in the air, and then over he rolled and lay still.

"'Great Heavens!' I said, 'why, you've hit him! He's dead.'

"As for Harry, he said nothing, but merely looked scared, as well he might, for such a marvellous, I may say such an appalling and ghastly fluke it has never been my lot to witness. A man, let alone a boy, might have fired a thousand such shots without ever touching the object; which, mind you, was springing and bounding over rocks quite five hundred yards away; and here this lad—taking a snap shot, and merely allowing for speed and elevation by instinct, for he did not put up his sights—had knocked the bull over as dead as a door-nail. Well, I made no further remark, as the occasion was too solemn for talking, but merely led the way to where the koodoo had fallen. There he lay, beautiful and quite still; and there, high up, about half-way down his neck, was a neat round hole. The bullet had severed the spinal marrow, passing through the vertebræ and away on the other side.

"It was already evening when, having cut as much of the best meat as we could carry from the bull, and tied a red handkerchief and some tufts of grass to his spiral horns, which, by the way, must have been nearly five feet in length, in the hope of keeping the jackals and aasvögels (vultures) from him, we finally got back to camp, to find Pharaoh, who was getting rather anxious at our absence, ready to greet us with the pleasing intelligence that another ox was sick. But even this dreadful bit of intelligence could not dash Harry's spirits; the fact of the matter being, incredible as it may appear, I do verily believe that in his heart of hearts he set down the death of the koodoo to the credit of his own skill. Now, though the lad was a pretty shot enough, this of course was ridiculous, and I told him so plainly.

"By the time that we had finished our supper of koodoo steaks (which would have been better if the koodoo had been a little younger), it was time to get ready for Jim-Jim's murderess. Accordingly we determined again to expose the unfortunate sick ox, that was now absolutely on its last legs, being indeed scarcely able to stand. All the afternoon Pharaoh told us it had been walking round and round in a circle as cattle in the last stage of redwater generally do. Now it had come to a standstill, and was swaying to and fro with its head hanging down. So we tied him up to the stump of the tree as on the previous night, knowing that if the lioness did not kill him he would be dead by morning. Indeed I was afraid that he would die at once, in which case he would be of but little use as a bait, for the lion is a sportsmanlike animal, and unless he is very hungry generally prefers to kill his own dinner, though when that is once killed he will come back to it again and again.

"Then we again went through our experience of the previous night, sitting there hour after hour, till at last Harry fell fast asleep, and, though I am accustomed to this sort of thing, even I could scarcely keep my eyes open. Indeed I was just dropping off, when suddenly Pharaoh gave me a push.

"'/Listen!/' he whispered.

"I was awake in a second, and listening with all my ears. From the clump of bush to the right of the lightning-shattered stump to which the sick ox was tied came a faint crackling noise. Presently it was repeated. Something was moving there, faintly and quietly enough, but still moving perceptibly, for in the intense stillness of the night any sound seemed loud.

"I woke up Harry, who instantly said, 'Where is she? where is she?' and began to point his rifle about in a fashion that was more dangerous to us and the oxen than to any possible lioness.

"'Be quiet!' I whispered, savagely; and as I did so, with a low and hideous growl a flash of yellow light sped out of the clump of bush, past the ox, and into the corresponding clump upon the other side. The poor sick creature gave a sort of groan, staggered round and then began to tremble. I could see it do so clearly in the moonlight, which was now very bright, and I felt a brute for having exposed the unfortunate animal to such agony as he must undoubtedly be undergoing. The lioness, for it was she, passed so quickly that we could not even distinguish her movements, much less fire. Indeed at night it is absolutely useless to attempt to shoot unless the object is very close and standing perfectly still, and then the light is so deceptive and it is so difficult to see the foresight that the best shot will miss more often than he hits.

"'She will be back again presently,' I said; 'look out, but for Heaven's sake don't fire unless I tell you to.'

"Hardly were the words out of my mouth when back she came, and again passed the ox without striking him.

"'What on earth is she doing?' whispered Harry.

"'Playing with it as a cat does with a mouse, I suppose. She will kill it presently.'

"As I spoke, the lioness once more flashed out of the bush, and this time sprang right over the doomed and trembling ox. It was a beautiful sight to see her clear him in the bright moonlight, as though it were a trick which she had been taught.

"'I believe that she has escaped from a circus,' whispered Harry; 'it's jolly to see her jump.'

29

"I said nothing, but I thought to myself that if it was, Master Harry did not quite appreciate the performance, and small blame to him. At any rate, his teeth were chattering a little.

"Then came a longish pause, and I began to think that the lioness must have gone away, when suddenly she appeared again, and with one mighty bound landed right on to the ox, and struck it a frightful blow with her paw.

"Down it went, and lay on the ground kicking feebly. She put down her wicked-looking head, and, with a fierce growl of contentment, buried her long white teeth in the throat of the dying animal. When she lifted her muzzle again it was all stained with blood. She stood facing us obliquely, licking her bloody chops and making a sort of purring noise.

"'Now's our time,' I whispered, 'fire when I do.'

"I got on to her as well as I could, but Harry, instead of waiting for me as I told him, fired before I did, and that of course hurried me. But when the smoke cleared, I was delighted to see that the lioness was rolling about on the ground behind the body of the ox, which covered her in such a fashion, however, that we could not shoot again to make an end of her.

"'She's done for! she's dead, the yellow devil!' yelled Pharaoh in exultation; and at that very moment the lioness, with a sort of convulsive rush, half-rolled, half-sprang, into the patch of thick bush to the right. I fired after her as she went, but so far as I could see without result; indeed the probability is that I missed her clean. At any rate she got to the bush in safety, and once there, began to make such a diabolical noise as I never heard before. She would whine and shriek with pain, and then burst out into perfect volleys of roaring that shook the whole place.

"'Well,' I said, 'we must just let her roar; to go into that bush after her at night would be madness.'

"At that moment, to my astonishment and alarm, there came an answering roar from the direction of the river, and then another from behind the swell of bush. Evidently there were more lions about. The wounded lioness redoubled her efforts, with the object, I suppose, of summoning the others to her assistance. At any rate they came, and quickly too, for within five minutes, peeping through the bushes of our skerm fence, we saw a magnificent lion bounding along towards us, through the tall tambouki grass, that in the moonlight looked for all the world like ripening corn. On he came in great leaps, and a glorious sight it was to see him. When within fifty yards or so, he stood still in an open space and roared. The lioness roared too; then there came a third roar, and another great black-maned lion stalked majestically up, and joined number two, till really I began to realize what the ox must have undergone.

"'Now, Harry,' I whispered, 'whatever you do don't fire, it's too risky. If they let us be, let them be.'

"Well, the pair marched off to the bush, where the wounded lioness was now roaring double tides, and the three of them began to snarl and grumble away together there. Presently, however, the lioness ceased roaring, and the two lions came out again, the black-maned one first—to prospect, I suppose—walked to where the carcass of the ox lay, and sniffed at it.

"'Oh, what a shot!' whispered Harry, who was trembling with excitement.

"'Yes,' I said; 'but don't fire; they might all of them come for us.'

"Harry said nothing, but whether it was from the natural impetuosity of youth, or because he was thrown off his balance by excitement, or from sheer recklessness and devilment, I am sure I cannot tell you, never having been able to get a satisfactory explanation from him; but at any rate the fact remains, he, without word or warning, entirely disregarding my exhortations, lifted up his Westley Richards and fired at

31

the black-maned lion, and, what is more, hit it slightly on the flank.

"Next second there was a most awful roar from the injured lion. He glared around him and roared with pain, for he was badly stung; and then, before I could make up my mind what to do, the great black-maned brute, clearly ignorant of the cause of his hurt, sprang right at the throat of his companion, to whom he evidently attributed his misfortune. It was a curious sight to see the astonishment of the other lion at this most unprovoked assault. Over he rolled with an angry snarl, and on to him sprang the black-maned demon, and began to worry him. This finally awoke the yellow-maned lion to a sense of the situation, and I am bound to say that he rose to it in a most effective manner. Somehow or other he got to his feet, and, roaring and snarling frightfully, closed with his mighty foe.

"Then ensued a most tremendous scene. You know what a shocking thing it is to see two large dogs fighting with abandonment. Well, a whole hundred of dogs could not have looked half so terrible as those two great brutes as they rolled and roared and rent in their horrid rage. They gripped each other, they tore at each other's throat, till their manes came out in handfuls, and the red blood streamed down their yellow hides. It was an awful and a wonderful thing to see the great cats tearing at each other with all the fierce energy of their savage strength, and making the night hideous with their heart-shaking noise. And the fight was a grand one too. For some minutes it was impossible to say which was getting the best of it, but at last I saw that the black-maned lion, though he was slightly bigger, was failing. I am inclined to think that the wound in his flank crippled him. Anyway, he began to get the worst of it, which served him right, as he was the aggressor. Still I could not help feeling sorry for him, for he had fought a gallant fight, when his antagonist finally got him by the throat, and, struggle and strike out as he would, began to shake the life out of him. Over and over they rolled together, a hideous and awe-inspiring spectacle, but the yellow one would not loose his hold, and at length poor black-mane grew faint, his breath came in great snorts and seemed to rattle in his nostrils, then he opened his huge mouth, gave the ghost of a roar, quivered, and was dead.

"When he was quite sure that the victory was his own, the yellow-maned lion loosed his grip and sniffed at the fallen foe. Then he licked the dead lion's eye, and next, with his fore-feet resting on the carcass, sent up his own chant of victory, that went rolling and pealing down the dark paths of the night. And at this point I interfered. Taking a careful sight at the centre of his body, in order to give the largest possible margin for error, I fired, and sent a .570 express bullet right through him, and down he dropped dead upon the carcass of his mighty foe.

"After that, fairly satisfied with our performances, we slept peaceably till dawn, leaving Pharaoh to keep watch in case any more lions should take it into their heads to come our way.

"When the sun was well up we arose, and went very cautiously—at least Pharaoh and I did, for I would not allow Harry to come—to see if we could find any trace of the wounded lioness. She had ceased roaring immediately upon the arrival of the two lions, and had not made a sound since, from which we concluded that she was probably dead. I was armed with my express, while Pharaoh, in whose hands a rifle was indeed a dangerous weapon, to his companions, had an axe. On our way we stopped to look at the two dead lions. They were magnificent animals, both of them, but their pelts were entirely spoiled by the terrible mauling they had given to each other, which was a sad pity.

"In another minute we were following the blood spoor of the wounded lioness into the bush, where she had taken refuge. This, I need hardly say, we did with the utmost caution; indeed,

I for one did not at all like the job, and was only consoled by the reflection that it was necessary, and that the bush was not thick. Well, we stood there, keeping as far from the trees as possible, searching and looking about, but no lioness could we see, though we saw plenty of blood.

"'She must have gone somewhere to die, Pharaoh,' I said in Zulu.

"'Yes, Inkoos,' he answered, 'she has certainly gone away.'

"Hardly were the words out of his mouth, when I heard a roar, and starting round saw the lioness emerge from the very centre of a bush, in which she had been curled up, just behind Pharaoh. Up she went on to her hind-legs, and as she did so I noticed that one of her fore- paws was broken near the shoulder, for it hung limply down. Up she went, towering right over Pharaoh's head, as she did so lifting her uninjured paw to strike him to the earth. And then, before I could get my rifle round or do anything to avert the oncoming catastrophe, the Zulu did a very brave and clever thing. Realizing his own imminent danger, he bounded to one side, and swinging the heavy axe round his head, brought it down right on to the back of the lioness, severing the vertebræ and killing her instantaneously. It was wonderful to see her collapse all in a heap like an empty sack.

"'My word, Pharaoh!' I said, 'that was well done, and none too soon.'

"'Yes,' he answered, with a little laugh, 'it was a good stroke, Inkoos. Jim-Jim will sleep better now.'

"Then, calling Harry to us, we examined the lioness. She was old, if one might judge from her worn teeth, and not very large, but thickly made, and must have possessed extraordinary vitality to have lived so long, shot as she was; for, in addition to her broken shoulder, my express bullet had blown a great hole in her middle that one might have put a fist into.

"Well, that is the story of the death of poor Jim-Jim and how we avenged it. It is rather interesting in its way, because of the fight between the two lions, of which I never saw the like in all my experience, and I know something of lions and their manners."

"And how did you get back to Pilgrim's Rest?" I asked Hunter Quatermain when he had finished his yarn.

"Ah, we had a nice job with that," he answered. "The second sick ox died, and so did another, and we had to get on as best we could with three harnessed unicorn fashion, while we pushed behind. We did about four miles a day, and it took us nearly a month, during the last week of which we pretty well starved."

"I notice," I said, "that most of your trips ended in disaster of some sort or another, and yet you went on making them, which strikes one as a little strange."

"Yes, I dare say: but then, remember I got my living for many years out of hunting. Besides, half the charm of the thing lay in the dangers and disasters, though they were terrible enough at the time. Another thing is, my trips were not all disastrous. Some time, if you like, I will tell you a story of one which was very much the reverse, for I made several thousand pounds out of it, and saw one of the most extraordinary sights a hunter ever came across. It was on this trip that I met the bravest native woman I ever knew; her name was Maiwa. But it is too late now, and besides, I am tired of talking about myself. Pass the water, will you!"

BOOMER BOOKS™

Readable Type
for People in their Prime

Boomer Books are not "large-print" books; they are books that are designed for comfortable reading, with ample line spacing, hanging punctuation, and superbly justified type. The typeface is Matthew Carter's Charter, which follows traditional old-style book types but with three differences: narrow proportions for economical use of space; a generous letter-height to improve readability; and sturdy, open letterforms that ensure legible printing in any environment. The result is a typeface that is handsome, versatile, and above all, readable. (The Boomer Books logo illustration is by Jazz Age artist John Held Jr.) We hope you enjoy Boomer Books! You'll find them all at www.boomer-books.biz.